# If you see a
# LION

For Ben and Jack – Be your own kind of cat! – K.N.

For Frieda, my little rabbit - A.S.

Quarto is the authority on a wide range of topics.

Quarto educates, entertains and enriches the lives of our readers—enthusiasts and lovers of hands-on living.

www.quartoknows.com

First published in 2020 by words & pictures,
an imprint of The Quarto Group.
The Old Brewery, 6 Blundell Street,
London N7 9BH, United Kingdom.
T (0)20 7700 6700 F (0)20 7700 8066
www.quartoknows.com

A catalogue record for this book is available from the British Library.

ISBN: 978 0 7112 5232 5

9 8 7 6 5 4 3 2 1

Manufactured in Guangzhou, China EB062020

MIX
Paper from responsible sources
FSC® C124385
www.fsc.org

words & pictures

# If you see a LION

Karl Newson          Andrea Stegmaier

Once upon a time, there was a story in this book.

FEARSOME KING

But a **LION** ate it all.

Orange,

furry,

handsome,

tall.

Once upon a time, a TOOT-ing
oompah band stood here...

TOOT!

But a lion ate them whole.

And a penguin

and a troll.

And a pirate and a wizard...
and a dinosaur as well!

**Mmm!**

If you see a lion, don't forget to yell!

Did *you* see a lion? Where?
No! I don't think so!
That's the pirate's hat,
not a lion. But, you know...

Once upon a time, there was a forest on this page...
But a lion nibbled it.

Every *itsy* *bitsy* bit.

Once upon a time, there was a dragon and a sprite.
But a lion took a bite in the middle of the night.

Then he swallowed up a river
and he chewed a mountain peak. Yum!

If you see a lion, don't forget to shriek!

**Eek!**

Did *someone* see a lion?
Where?
Ha! I don't think so!

That's the dragon's gold, not a lion! But, you know...
There has to be a lion hiding *somewhere* in this book.

Dreamy, clever, awesome, strong.

Come in *closer* for a look...

Once upon a time, there was an *A, B, C* on here...
But a lion chomped it down...

Then a hippo,

then a clown.

HA!

Once upon a time, there was a unicorn up there.

But a lion licked it clean.
Now there's nothing to be seen.

Then he snacked upon
a doughnut
and a pumpkin
and a sprout.

Blergh!

If you see a lion,
don't forget to...

LION!

Hello, little rabbit!
Was it *you* who called me so?

I was looking for a *snack*...
How nice of you to say hello!

Hop into my mouth, I'll keep you safe from
**You-know-who**...

YOU MUST BE ROARING MAD!

We know the lion is **YOU!**

You gobbled up the oompah band,
the penguin
and the troll.
The pirate and the wizard
and the dinosaur – **WHOLE!**
It was *you* who ate the forest
and the dragon
and the sprite!
The river
and the mountain peak in

# ONE. BIG. BITE!

The A, B, C of everything,
the hippo
and the clown.
You didn't lick the unicorn…
YOU SWALLOWED IT RIGHT DOWN!

You chowed upon the doughnut

and the pumpkin

and the sprout.

You gobbled up my friends,
but I've come to

**get**

**them**

**out!**

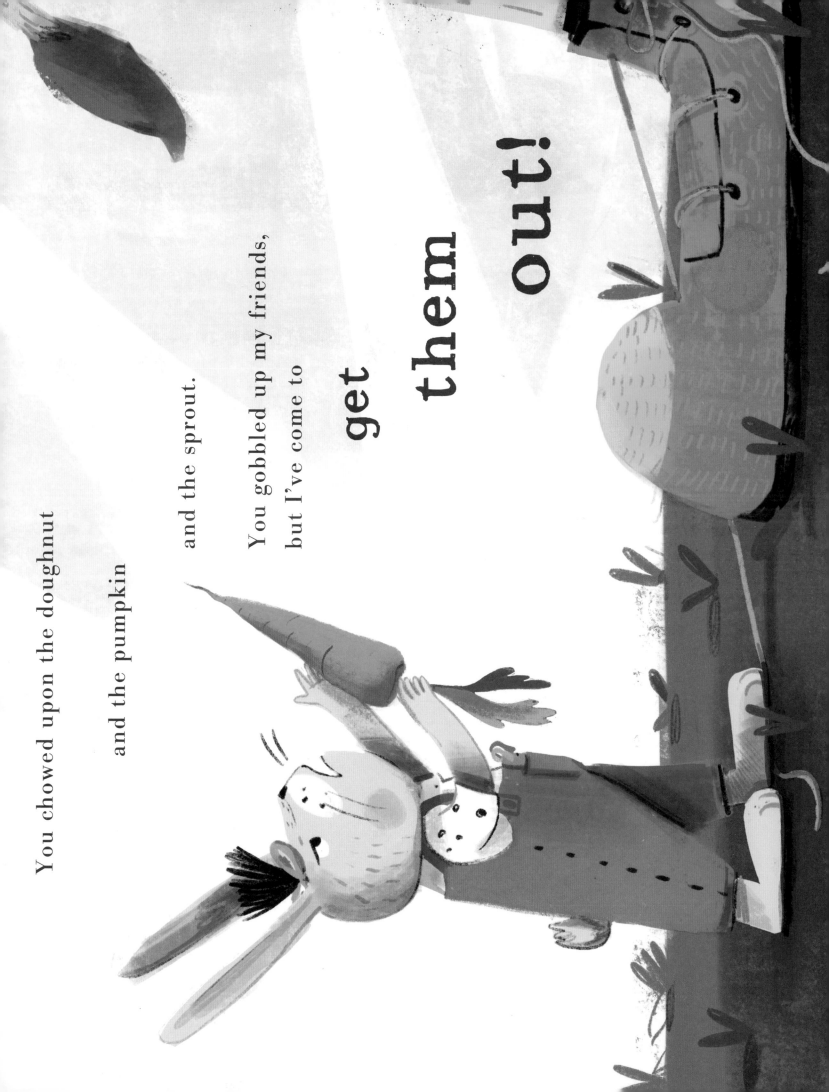

Did *you* see where the rabbit went?

Once upon a...

OOH!

No? Well, never mind...
You and I are here,
and there's a lion
we must find!

There was a....

**AAH!**

There was a....

# STOP!
## NO MORE HOPPING, RABBIT!

You're gonna make me...

Uh-oh...

POP!

What's your story, Lion?
Why'd you eat up *everything*?

*Why?* Because I can of course!
That's why they call me King.

But you could just be YOU!
You could be your own kind of cat.

Like Dragon – she
won't char us all

and Troll won't
squash us flat.

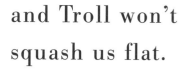

It's OK being you...
Be like the lion in your heart!
We'd love you all the same,
there's no need to play a part.

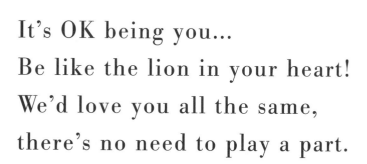

But if I don't eat EVERYTHING...
Well, then my cover's blown.
You'd never call me King,
I'd be useless and alone.

Nonsense! You'd have all of us. And even better still...
You'd be *King of Fancy Dress*! Come join us? Say you will?

Once upon a time, there was a lion in this book...
And he led the big parade!
(Yes, I'm really glad I stayed.)

I'm the king of being me!
And I'm super in myself –
I've made the best of friends,
inside this book, upon your shelf.

But every now and then,
I just can't help a little gnaw...
So if you see a lion...

KING OF BEING
ME!

Don't forget to

# ROAR!

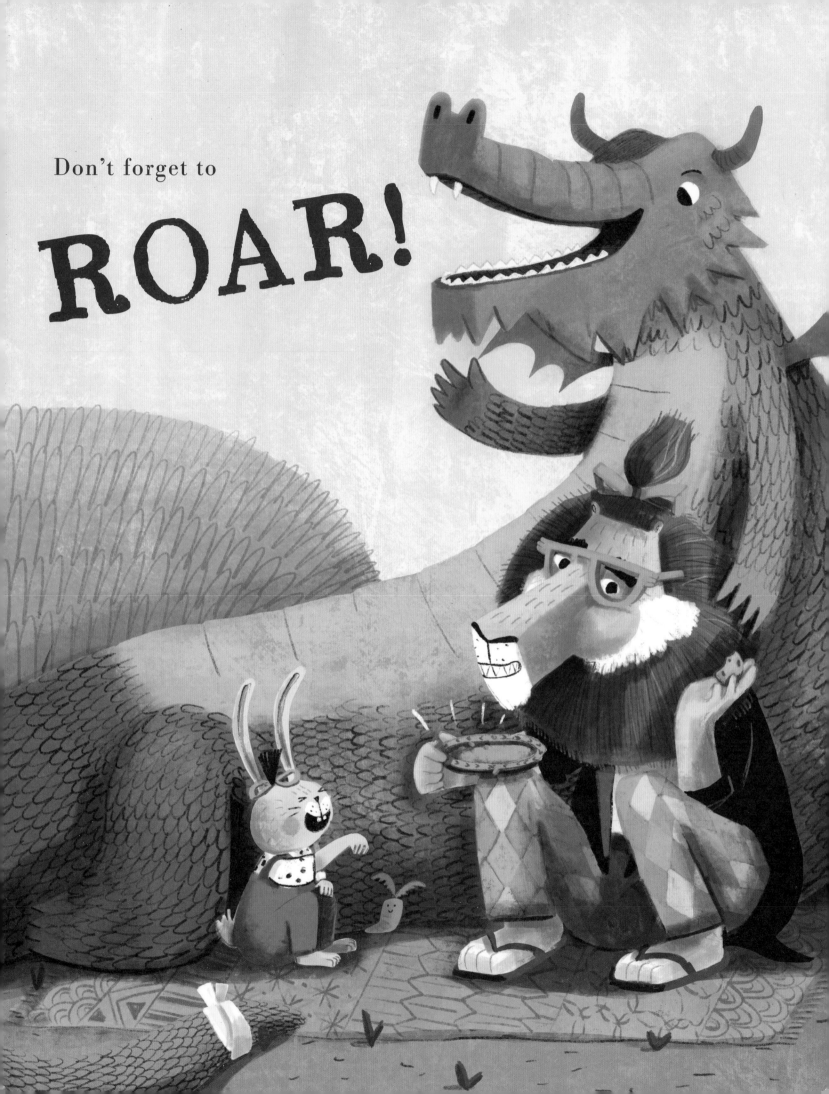